Yesterday I Had the BLUES

To Sheri—it still is and always will be yours.
—J.F.

For Garcelle, Sonriza, Howard, and Lidia.
Thanks for the exposure to Dutch love, fun, and culture.
See you in Amsterdam.
—"Christie"

Text copyright © 2003 by Jeron Ashford Frame
Illustrations copyright © 2003 by R. Gregory Christie

All rights reserved. Published in the United States by Tricycle Press, an imprint
of the Crown Publishing Group, a division of Random House, Inc., New York.
www.crownpublishing.com
www.tricyclepress.com

Tricycle Press and the Tricycle Press colophon are registered trademarks
of Random House, Inc.

Library of Congress Cataloging-in-Publication Data

Frame, Jeron Ashford.
  Yesterday I had the blues / by Jeron Ashford Frame ; illustrations by
R. Gregory Christie.
      p. cm.
Summary: A young boy ponders a variety of emotions and how different
members of his family experience them, from his own blues to his
father's grays and his grandmother's yellows.

  [1. Emotions--Fiction. 2. Family life--Fiction. 3. African
Americans--Fiction.] I. Christie, Gregory, 1971-, ill. II. Title.
  PZ7.F8445 Ye 2003
  [E]--dc21
                                         2002155295
ISBN 978-1-58246-084-0 hardcover
ISBN 978-1-58246-260-8 paperback

Printed in China

Design by Betsy Stromberg
Typeset in Spleeny Decaf
The illustrations in this book were rendered in acrylic and gouache.

13 — 15

First Edition

Yesterday I Had the BLUES

by Jeron Ashford Frame

Illustrations by R. Gregory Christie

TRICYCLE PRESS
Berkeley

Yesterday I had the
blues.

Not the rain on the sidewalk blues,
or the broken skateboard blues, or the
outgrew my favorite football jersey blues.

Not even the Monday mornin'
cold cereal instead of pancakes blues.

Uh-uh,

I had those deep down in my shoes blues,
the go away, Mr. Sun, quit smilin' at me blues.

The hold a pillow,
wish it was tomorrow blues.

The kind of blues
make you wanna just

turn

down

the

volume.

But today I got the
greens.

The runnin' my hand along the hedges greens.

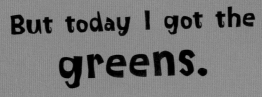

The down to the drugstore
and beyond,
dirt in my socks
greens.

The kind of
greens make you
want to be Somebody.

The don't ask for a new skateboard till tomorrow grays.

Poor Daddy.

Sasha says she got the
pinks.

The shiny tights,
ballet after school,
glitter on her cheeks pinks.

The where's my butterfly hair clip? pinks.

The kind of pinks
make me
want to catch the next bus.

Talia says she got the **indigos.**

I said, indigo's the same as blue.

Talia says, uh-uh,
she got the saxophone
in the subway
indigos.

The hair hangin' loose,
write a poem that don't rhyme indigos.

The kind of indigos
make her act
like the drapes.

Gram's got the **yellows**, I can tell.

The hummin' that parade song,
flower house slipper yellows.

The mix up some
oatmeal raisin cookies
                              (I hope)
yellows.

Mama
says
she
got
the
reds.

Look out!

Yeah, yesterday I had the
blues.

Today I got the
greens.

Tomorrow maybe it'll be the
silvers.

The rocket-powered skateboard silvers!

And around here, that's okay.
'Cause together we got somethin'
that'll never change.

We got a family—
the kind of family makes you feel
like it's

all

golden.

JERON ASHFORD FRAME was listening to a blues song on her car radio when she came up with the idea to write *Yesterday I Had the Blues*. When she's not writing, Jeron works at an academic library and spends time with her three daughters and her cat, Boomer. She lives near Philadelphia, Pennsylvania.

R. GREGORY CHRISTIE is a three-time recipient of the Coretta Scott King Honor Award. He has illustrated over twenty picturebooks and contributes regularly to the *New Yorker* and other magazines. Gregory works out of his studio in Brooklyn, New York. Visit www.gas-art.com.